COFFEE CAKE AND CALAMITIES

A BELLE HARBOR COZY MYSTERY
(BOOK 7)

SUE HOLLOWELL

CONTENTS

CHAPTER ONE

The announcement from the loudspeaker instructed us to wait behind the yellow line while the train entered the station. The early morning marine layer was heavy enough to blot out the view of the ocean and any glimpse of sun. I had high hopes for the fog to lift by the time we were on our trip. The pictures of the view from the Coast Excursion were spectacular. On the east side of the train, lightly snow-capped mountain peaks bordered much of the trip. On the west side, the ocean ran as far as the eye could see. In many places along the route, the train ran high up on rocky cliffs.

The train squeaked to a stop in front of us, bellowing and moaning as it settled in to open the doors for passengers to embark.

I tightly gripped the handle on my overnight case with wheels by my side. Uncle Jack, Linda, Justin, and I planned this trip as a last hurrah before my dream come true of the grand opening of Luna's Bakery and Cafe. Once we opened the doors, it would be quite some time before I would be able to venture out for more than a few hours at a time. Unkie and Linda huddled together, heads bowed toward each other. Those two had become almost inseparable since they had met.

How the universe had guided Uncle Jack to run Linda's estate sale, I would never know. His Checkered Past Antiques shop occupied most of his waking time, when he wasn't also looking out for me. But something in the air prompted him to agree, and I couldn't be happier for the two of them. He did, however, vow to never do that again. And fate wasn't done with Linda and our family, as she had quite the baking skills. She was more than my assistant. Our collaboration and strategy for running Luna's elevated her position to that of an operations manager. I shook my head, still in awe that I had my own small business. With employees. The real deal. My persistence toward my vision, and a heavy and consistent dose of encouragement from Uncle Jack, had resulted in my very own place.

"Can I get that for you?" Justin asked, extending his arm to grab my bag. The crowd edged forward toward the conductor, checking tickets as we boarded the train. I stepped back and allowed Justin to hoist the bag up the steps. I held the handrail and followed him to the car on our left. He heaved my bag up to the overhead bin. "Did you bring a pile of bricks with you?" he asked as he huffed, shoving it back toward the wall. "You have quite the weapon if you need it."

I chuckled, noticing Justin's straining bicep as he placed his bag next to mine. His form-fitting T-shirt showed off his athletic body. Along with owning his own business, his passion was surfing. Or really any kind of water sports. One of my fondest memories was our kayak trip fiasco. His embarrassment at shoving me off by myself without paddles was still prevalent to this day. He did redeem himself with another trip. We spent a long afternoon paddling throughout the bay, observing the quaint, small town of Belle Harbor from the water.

Scanning the car, I saw that seats were filling fast. I quickly scooted to the last row and nabbed the only two remaining together. I moved to the window and patted the seat next to me for Justin to sit. He plopped down, his light blond curls bouncing just a smidgen.

My time since arriving in Belle Harbor had been consumed with starting my bakery and re-starting my life. To have a place to safely land after the disaster with my ex-husband was nothing short of a minor miracle. And the people surrounding me were becoming like family. Justin rented the room above Unkie's antique shop and was a constant presence in our lives, along with his cat Willie, who became an unexpected father with the bookstore owner's cat Gwinnie. Even more wonderful from that pairing was my unforeseen adoption of one of their kittens. My Peanut had become a constant companion.

"Don't worry. I'm sure it'll clear any minute now," Justin said.

I turned my gaze from the window toward him. "Huh?"

"Wow, you were a million miles away," he said.

The wall of windows on both sides of the train extended overhead. You could recline your seat and watch the sky pass by. I closed my eyes, imagining the night with twinkling stars and the moon overhead. The train jolted forward, launching us into our adventure.

"Thanks for coming," I said.

Linda had convinced Uncle Jack to take this trip. But truth be told, it wasn't much of a hard sell. They wouldn't take no for an answer when they asked me to join them, knowing I wouldn't have a break from my new cafe for quite some time. There was still so much to do before opening, I only hoped I could enjoy my time on this short jaunt. Not wanting to feel like a third wheel, I asked Justin along. He eagerly accepted. With his response I hoped he hadn't gotten the wrong idea. I was nowhere near ready for a romantic relationship. He and I enjoyed a companionship in exploring and experiencing Belle Harbor and the surrounding areas, but that needed to be the extent of it.

The motion of the train settled into a gentle rocking as it got up to speed.

"I've always wanted to take this trip," Justin said. He reached his arm across me to point out a rock formation in the water. "That's called a sea stack." Three rocks sat just offshore like tiny islands. Not much more was visible from the fog beyond them. "That particular location is also a national wildlife refuge to protect the nesting sea birds and sea lions."

Squinting, I peered out the window to spot any of the creatures. A few birds circled the rocks, landing and taking off again. The train, now up to speed and rumbling along, could have lulled me to sleep. The early departure was necessary in order to fit in all of the stops along our trip.

"What do you say we go get some coffee?" I asked.

Justin stood and held his hand to guide me to the aisle. I took it briefly as I rose from my seat, pondering his intent with that gesture. He had a gentle and kind demeanor. But I wondered if he was secretly hoping for more in our relationship. Time would tell.

"Unkie, Linda, would you like something from the dining car?" I asked as Justin and I stood in the aisle next to the lovebirds.

Uncle Jack looked at Linda. She shook her head. "I'm OK for now. But thank you for asking," she said.

"We'll be back in a bit." I led the way through the passenger cars to where I could smell the aroma of caffeine beckoning me.

We passed through four cars full of people on our way. Each car with the expansive windows provided the feeling of floating along the tracks above the ocean. The dining car had booths lining both sides with only a few tables occupied. Justin held out his hand to inquire if a table met my approval. We took a seat as the server arrived. "Welcome to the Coast Excursion. What can I get you?" She looked back and forth between Justin and me.

"I'll start with coffee," I said. "Black."

"Same," Justin said.

"You got it. I'll have that right up for you." She noted our order on her pad and put it in her pocket, tucking the pencil behind her ear.

"I can't believe how beautiful the scenery is. And it looks so different from this vantage point," I said, gazing out the window. This trip was just what I needed. A forced distance from my business for a bit. I was already starting to relax.

"Cathy, would you leave it alone?" a deep voice behind me hissed.

My head snapped up and my eyes widened. Justin leaned slightly to his right to see over my shoulder.

"I wish I could," Cathy responded. "Every time I see that woman in the office, it comes back to me," she replied.

"Seriously, you've made out pretty well with this deal," the male voice said. "I'm the one who's had to deal with disposing of the trash."

"I guess. I'm just glad it'll be gone before we get back from our trip," Cathy replied.

CHAPTER TWO

Justin's eyes bulged. He leaned forward and whispered so quietly I almost couldn't hear. "That's weird. What do you think they're talking about?"

I shook my head, insistent I wouldn't get involved in anything except my happiness and relaxation on this trip. "Maybe we should just get our coffee to go and head back," I suggested.

Turning, I saw the waitress arriving with a tray holding our two steaming mugs of coffee. Well, maybe we could be fast about it. In my quick glance I saw Cathy and the man with her two tables away from us, who seemed pretty relaxed at their table. Maybe we misunderstood what they were talking about.

Justin and I sat back as the waitress placed the cups in front of us. We smiled up at her as she tucked the tray under her arm. "Let me know if you'd like anything else," she offered and exited our table.

I pulled my cup toward me, focusing on the dark brown liquid jostling with the movement of the train. I tried to block out whatever was going on behind me.

Lifting my head, I said, "I think the thing I'm most excited about on this trip is the bed and breakfast. In their online listing, they talk about their award-winning coffee cake."

Justin nodded. "Uh huh." He continued to stretch his neck, peering over my shoulder.

Gazing out the window, watching the scenery rush by, I secretly hoped for no drama on this trip. My nerves over the last several months were pretty fried due to the remodel of my bakery. My vision had come to life, but birthing that baby was no easy feat.

The train jolted, sloshing some of our coffee onto the table. I stood. "I'll grab some napkins," I said, heading toward the supply station.

Passing by the couple's table, I saw they had ordered breakfast. They appeared to be middle-aged. The man was burly, big arms, dark, stringy hair, long enough to put into a ponytail. The woman, Cathy, was petite. Their heads were buried in their food, oblivious to anyone else.

I pulled a handful of napkins from the dispenser and returned to my table, setting the pile onto the pool of coffee.

Shaking his head, Justin said, "I'm glad we're doing this too."

"Curtis, are you sure the destruction is happening on schedule?" Cathy asked.

If their conversation was referring to something nefarious, why would they be so public with it? Dropping into the middle of a discussion could lead your brain to all kinds of wrong conclusions.

"Yes. Now quit nagging me about it. You know I've been in this business forever. I know how it runs," Curtis responded.

Justin brought his cup to his mouth, in a daze, focused intently on the couple behind me.

"Do you think anyone will be suspicious about why Paula didn't come on the trip?" Cathy asked.

"Seriously, shut your trap now," Curtis ordered.

Silence ensued; the only sound was silverware hitting plates. Family drama was the worst. People treated their relatives in ways they wouldn't treat their worst enemies.

"Let's finish up and head back." I rose and paused, seeing another couple arriving in the dining car.

The May-December couple gazed into each other's eyes as if they were on a honeymoon. That's more like what I wanted to see. People enjoying each other and life. They passed by our table and chose seats on the side opposite Curtis and Cathy.

"Hey Dad. Hey Sandra," Curtis said, clearing his throat.

"This is so lovely," Sandra said.

Justin placed his elbows on the table, his head turning back and forth between the two couples like he was watching a tennis match.

I heard the waitress approach the new couple's table, inquiring for their beverage order. Part of me wanted to join Justin on the other side of the table to watch the show. The other part wanted to jet as far away from the place as possible. I closed my eyes, envisioning Uncle Jack and Linda, two of the most non-dramatic and nicest people on the planet.

"I'm so glad we could all come," Sandra said.

"Well, not all of us," Cathy chimed in.

Her snide remarks kept on coming. Was she going to reveal what was really going on? Maybe we should order food to stick around a bit longer.

"Cathy!" Curtis yelled. He seemed to have no qualms about making a scene in public.

"And closing down the company so we could take this trip was absurd," Cathy said. That woman spoke her mind. For better or worse.

"You know," Sandra started. She lowered her voice and continued, "This might be the last family get together we will have before..." Her voice trailed off.

"It's fine, Sandra. You can say it. I'm ready to go," the man said.

Her voice stuttering, Sandra said, "Raymond." She continued in a stronger tone. "Don't ruin it for him, you two," she ordered.

All talking stopped, and I heard plates of food being placed on the table.

"Justin," I said, hoping this lull would be a good time to escape.

"I'm just glad Paula is taking some time for herself, finally," Sandra started up again. "You could stand to be nicer to your sister, Curtis," she admonished.

The waitress arrived with a pot of coffee, refilled our cups, and removed the pile of sopping napkins. I settled in to be here for a while longer.

"She's the one who's the chief operations officer. I'm just a lowly tow truck driver," he sniveled.

"Curtis, you know why we did that." Raymond finally arrived to the fracas. The old man's voice sounded as shaky as he looked. My age estimator was usually way off, but no doubt he was at least eighty. Maybe more. Sandra couldn't have been more than half his age. To each their own. I wasn't going to judge.

"Curtis, I told you to get out of that tow truck and go back to school," Cathy chimed in.

"He never let me," Curtis whined. "Always said I was the best driver."

"Stop it!" Sandra yelled. "You're ruining this trip!"

I stood, ready for this to be over. "Justin, let's go."

I grabbed both of our cups and headed to a bin for dirty dishes. We had only finished about half of our second cups, but I was done. I gently placed them inside and reached for Justin's hand, sure if I didn't lead him from the dining car he might stay until our stop at the winery. At the other end of the car, the other couple who were there when we arrived bowed their heads toward each other. They would have to pass by the feuding family in order to leave, and it looked like they had chosen to wait it out.

"Sorry, Dad," Curtis offered, a conciliatory tone in his voice, his head bowing.

Maybe they would all get along for the sake of Raymond, whatever was going on with him. If he was sick, I really hoped the family could provide him with some lovely memories before he passed. That must be heart-wrenching to know your loved one's days were literally numbered. And if that didn't prompt you to change your behavior, I didn't know what would.

CHAPTER THREE

I exited the dining car to return to Linda and Uncle Jack and sped along the path.

"Tilly, wait up," Justin said.

I turned, stopping mid-aisle. Justin almost bumped into me, grabbing my hand as we took a couple of vacant seats nearby.

"Justin, my gut is not liking this at all. I really hope it's nothing but family drama. But..." I faced the window, gazing at the mountain range with snow-capped peaks. The beauty of the jagged hills was breathtaking. My mind drifted to consider another adventure with Justin. Perhaps a hike.

Justin leaned over to me, glancing around at the smattering of passengers in the car. "Tilly, let's just take one step at a time. For now, we've got the winery tour coming up." He leaned his head back and closed his eyes, inhaling deeply. I admired his ability to chill in the most stressful of moments.

The surrounding windows allowed the emerging sun to warm the cars. The brightening day boosted my mood, and it didn't hurt to be surrounded by my favorite people.

We sat for several minutes, my blood pressure returning somewhat to normal. My brain seemed to naturally consider scandalous behavior when hearing tidbits like we did from Curtis and Cathy. I tried to maneuver my thoughts into a space where there could be a logical explanation for their words. Shoving that rationale to the back of my mind to ruminate, I said, "You're right. Let's head back to Jack and Linda."

Justin stood and led the way back to our original car.

We entered and returned to our seats to await the upcoming stop at the Pacific Coast Winery. The brochure pictures depicted views overlooking the ocean cliffs, a perfect place for an ocean wedding. If my hopes for a union between Unkie and Linda came true, maybe they would consider this venue. Our visit would be a trial run of the place, at least in my mind.

"Tilly." Uncle Jack stood, looking between Justin and me. "What's wrong?"

Oh, boy. Wearing my emotions on my sleeve gave me away. I shook my head. "Nothing. Just settling in for the trip."

Unkie looked at Justin, not buying my answer one bit. Justin shrugged. "She's stubborn."

I glared at Justin.

"I mean, persistent," Justin continued, smirking. He gestured toward our seats.

He was right. Stubborn it was. But one thing I was learning about myself was to trust my instincts. Every time I deviated from what my gut was telling me, I ended up being wrong. Every. Time.

We sat in the row behind Unkie and Linda. Peeking back between the seats, Uncle Jack asked, "OK. I know you won't let it rest until you get answers. What's going on?"

Our train car was full, passengers either gazing out at the scenery or heads buried in devices. For better or worse, the Coast Excursion provided free Wi-fi so you could surf the internet in between stops.

Leaning forward, I provided Uncle Jack with a summary of our observations. "I don't know what it is exactly, but the details we overheard made it sound like at least two people conspiring to get rid of a body."

Uncle Jack glanced at Justin and back at me. "Well, all I ask is please be careful not to get mixed up in something dangerous. We're here for relaxation, and I really hope you will take advantage of this wonderful opportunity." Unkie returned to his position to chat with Linda.

He wasn't wrong and never pulled any punches saying his piece. Could I let this go and solely focus on the moment to enjoy this spectacular trip? I reached under the seat in front of me and extracted my backpack, putting it on my lap. Maybe if I jotted down my thoughts I could release them and put all of this aside for a while.

With pen and notebook in hand I began my typical process to make sense of the information I had. A circle in the center of the page had no name, for now. Was there even a victim? And if so, what was the crime? Cathy and Curtis spoke in code about getting rid of the trash. I listed their names around the center circle, drawing a line between the two. I wrote "spouse" on the line. After a second thought, I added "conspiracy" to the line. They were both in on something, and I needed to find out what that something was.

Sitting back in my seat, I looked at Justin. He pointed to my paper and said, "Raymond and Sandra."

I smiled. Apparently he concluded that if you can't beat 'em, join 'em. Granted, he may just be humoring me for the time being. No matter, I would take it. I added the two names and drew a connecting line indicating "spouse." It was obvious Sandra was quite a bit younger than Raymond, which meant she was not the mother to

Curtis. Another line on my page connecting Curtis and Raymond as parent/child. Off to the side, I wrote "trash." Someone named Paula wasn't on the trip but by all indications was smack dab in the middle of this mystery. She got a spot on the page along with "business--tow company."

Curtis's resentful tone about his position in the company might be the key to explaining this drama. I wrote the word "bitter" next to Curtis. His wife Cathy appeared to be in cahoots with whatever he had going on, but there was something additional between her and Curtis. Something she wouldn't let Curtis forget. I wrote "woman" on the page and "office." The entire piece of paper was now filled with circles and lines but with no apparent pattern to enlighten the path to answers.

I tucked the pen and paper into my backpack. With my thoughts out of my brain, perhaps I could focus on fun.

Leaning over to me, Justin cupped his hand in front of his mouth and whispered, "Let's sit close by Curtis and Cathy at the wine tasting. Maybe we can put this mystery to bed once and for all."

Was he tolerating my nuttiness or truly on board with sleuthing? It was easy to get caught up in solving the unanswered questions, at least for me. I liked logic and explanations, fitting all of the pieces of the puzzle together to paint a clear picture.

Justin leaned his seat back and closed his eyes. I admired his ability to chill out, even in the midst of stress and uncertainty. I followed suit and closed my eyes, hoping to turn off my thoughts. I nudged him with my elbow. "Thank you," I said.

He chuckled. My heart warmed with his response. My friends and family got me.

I turned toward the window, unable to get into a state of leisure. I envisioned the setup at the winery to decide how best to sidle up to Curtis and Cathy. The brochure described round tables situated on a large lawn for the tasting, each seating about eight people. Justin and I needed to be among the first to depart to survey our options. I would navigate us toward the center to wait for the duo to disembark. That way we would have the shortest distance to tail them to a table without appearing as if we were stalking them. At least I hoped that would work. How did I get to be so conniving with my intent?

The rumble of the train soothed my nerves a bit as the nature scenery whizzed by on our way to our destination.

CHAPTER FOUR

The engine of the train geared down as we slowed toward the station. All of the passengers in our car stood as the motion jostled us until we came to a full stop. I hooked my backpack strap over my shoulder as Justin and I entered the aisle. The door slid open, revealing a long driveway leading to the winery. I panned the crowd, shading my eyes as I searched for our targets.

Justin jetted to the center of the crowd, in a good position to spot Curtis and Cathy. I dashed after him, hoping I didn't draw too much attention, other than people thinking I was eager for a good seat for the wine tasting.

Not hard to find, Curtis stood about a head taller than most of the other guests. Justin and I kept about ten feet behind him as we all ambled toward our destination. A small shuttle bus arrived to transport those guests needing some assistance. I glanced over at Uncle Jack and pointed at it. He pursed his lips and shook his head. *Not that I think you're elderly, Unkie.*

Looking up ahead, I saw that we had about the length of a football field to go. To each side of us were vineyards as far as the eye could see. The elevation of the property provided views of the ocean in front of us and the mountain range to the rear. I felt like we were walking to the end of the earth.

As the open space came into view, I could see quite a few tables spread out on a lawn, just like the pictures in the brochure. I elbowed Justin and slightly bobbed my head in the direction of Curtis and Cathy. We followed them in lockstep to a table on the right, just outside what looked like a barn. I hadn't spotted any animals, so it must have been a storage shed for all of the farm equipment.

"How about this one?" Justin gestured to the table where Curtis and Cathy were already seated.

Smooth move. Let the sleuthing continue. "This is great," I said, placing my backpack under my seat. "We've got a good view of the ocean too."

About three tables in front of us, Uncle Jack and Linda had somehow gotten seated at the same table as Raymond and Sandra. With a slight glance my way, Unkie winked at me. *Yes!* We would have to compare notes later. I didn't think he could resist diving into a juicy puzzle.

"This is beautiful. Hi, I'm Tilly." I reached my arm over to shake hands with Curtis and Cathy. For what seemed like an awkward amount of time, my arm hung in front of Curtis. He looked at it like I was offering him a dead fish.

Finally giving it a token shake, he said, "Curtis. This is Cathy." He tilted his head to his right.

Cathy sat back in her chair, shoulders slumped and arms crossed in front of her. She made no eye contact with us. My only hope at this stage was that the wine would loosen them up. Two other couples joined our table, introducing themselves.

Everyone was now seated and the speaker was moving to the front of the group. She welcomed us to the Pacific Coast Winery, explaining how the tasting would work. Servers would be roaming around the tables to provide samples of six different wines. The speaker described each of the varieties we would try.

Under his breath, Curtis mumbled, "Just get on with it." He sat forward with elbows on the table.

Gritting her teeth, Cathy replied, "Can you just try to enjoy it? I've been wanting to do this for a long time, and you're not going to ruin it for me."

The other couples at our table glanced at each other, likely questioning their choice of company. Sadly for them, there were no other open seats to escape to.

Curtis held up his arm like he was signaling a waiter. The server made eye contact and continued to the table next to ours. Curtis harrumphed impatiently, tapping his fingers on his empty glass.

The wine server approached our table and started with Curtis, explaining in further detail about the specific wine that was first up in the tasting. "Fill it up," Curtis ordered. The server looked at him and then around to each of us.

"We provide a sample for tasting. We've got six different varieties today," the server explained.

"I don't care. Fill it up," Curtis repeated and threw a twenty dollar bill on the table.

The server poured a tad more into Curtis's glass and made his way around the table to provide the rest of us our share.

Cathy grabbed her glass and swigged it down in one gulp. The other couples at the table looked at each other, trying to make sense of what was happening. Little did they know there was much more than met the eye.

Curtis slumped in his chair like a petulant child.

"I think I can taste the cherries in this one," Justin interjected. Yes, we were here for wine tasting.

I held out my glass, looking at the ruby red liquid. I knew nothing about wine, but I agreed it did have a hint of cherries.

Following the wine servers, the food began to arrive. Small nibbles to cleanse our palates between the wines. The sequence continued with the second wine arriving.

Curtis grabbed the server by the arm and said, "Leave the bottle." He threw a few more twenties onto the table, next to the one already there.

"Sir--" the server began.

Curtis raised his arm in a *talk to the hand* way. The server rounded the table, providing us all our portions, explaining the oak flavor notes in this variety, and set the bottle in front of Curtis.

"Seriously, you think you can just buy people off?" Cathy asked. She reached for the bottle, and Curtis moved it out of her reach. If this continued, we would have to wheel them back to the train. Four more samples to go.

I placed a serving of bruschetta onto my plate, eager to busy myself with something. Not many clues from those two at the moment, except Curtis throwing around money like he could buy everyone off.

"It's worked so far, hasn't it?" Curtis retorted. "This trip wouldn't be possible without me, so I don't want to hear another word."

This was getting extremely uncomfortable. I would have to rethink my approach for clue gathering from now on to make sure I had an exit strategy.

I turned my chair toward the two other couples at our table, hoping a distraction might ease the tension. "What activities are you planning to do at the bed and breakfast?" I asked.

The woman to Justin's left quickly glanced toward Curtis and Cathy and said, "We were thinking to try the stand-up paddle boarding on the lake."

"Us too," Justin added. "I love the water."

The wine server approached with bottle number three. This time, he started pouring at the opposite side of the table from Curtis, explaining the next tasting was a holiday flavor with Christmas spices. The pile of bills remained awkwardly between Curtis and Cathy. As the server navigated around the table, Curtis shoved the bills in his direction, indicating for him to leave bottle number three in front of him. This was getting to be a pattern.

Justin continued to chat up the other table guests, trying for some semblance of normalcy. With this fiasco, I was sure those couples would steer as far away from Curtis and Cathy as humanly possible

for the remainder of our trip.

CHAPTER FIVE

We were halfway through the tastings, and Unkie and Linda were yukking it up at their table. The sun was now directly overhead, bathing us all in warmth. I grabbed the ice-water pitcher from the middle of the table and filled my glass. Two platters with the second set of nibbles arrived at our table, containing small skewers of chicken, melon, and cheese. Curtis reached first and grabbed a handful, plunking them on the plate in front of him. That guy had no manners whatsoever. The rest of us, including Cathy, passed and shared the food from the second platter, leaving the other to Curtis.

He appeared to be oblivious to how his behavior was perceived by the rest of the table. He grabbed the bottle next to him and filled his glass to the brim.

"Tilly, what do you think about that?" Justin asked.

My focus was so fixed on Curtis's astonishing behavior, I had lost touch of the conversation happening on the other side of the table. I shook my head to reset my thoughts.

I placed my left hand on Justin's arm to center myself. "I'm sorry," I said.

"You were deep in thought. What about the cider-making activity at the B&B?" Justin asked.

"Mm-hmm. Sounds like fun." I was really ready for anything to help me escape for a while.

"Oooo, Curtis. Let's do that," Cathy said, joining the conversation.

I shifted in my seat to bring Cathy further into the discussion. Perhaps fixing my attention on her would prove more fruitful.

"That sounds ridiculous," Curtis replied, gulping from his glass.

"You're welcome to join us if you'd like," I offered. Curtis could just be on his own. Maybe separating the two of them was a good strategy to poke further into this mystery.

"I would. Thank you." Cathy sneered at Curtis. She had no qualms at speaking her piece.

Away from Curtis I hoped she would sing like a canary. Exploring the reason for the rift between them could prove beneficial in understanding more clues.

Curtis sniffed, keeping his eyes on his plate. He picked up the wine bottle and tipped it up over his glass. A few drops emptied the remaining amount. He stood, looking around for the server, holding up the empty bottle. I wondered if the owners had ever had a customer before that acted as poorly and entitled as Curtis. Probably, but I hoped for their sake it was few and far between. He plunked into his seat and slammed the bottle on the table, causing the entire group to jump in unison.

The server arrived at our table with the fourth wine for sampling. Again, he began pouring for everyone except Curtis, glaring at him, daring him to speak. If not for the major distraction of sleuthing and Curtis's deplorable behavior I would be thoroughly enjoying myself. The winery setting was unparalleled. The breeze from the ocean cooled us just enough not to bake in the midday heat.

A younger man I hadn't seen before now quickly approached our table from behind the server. His tall, lanky frame tromped up, his arm outstretched with a finger pointed at Curtis. Oh boy. Buckle up for act two. "You," he started.

I looked at Justin, his eyebrows raised. I leaned over and whispered to him, "Do you know who that is?"

Justin shook his head.

"Get out of here, Jamie," Curtis said. He grabbed a skewer and slid the food into his mouth, tossing the stick onto the plate.

Circling the table toward Curtis, Jamie said, "I won't let this go. You're the reason my mom took off." He raised his voice, drawing attention from the nearby tables. Great, now this show was the center of attention. So much for stealthily seeking clues.

I squeezed my eyes shut, imprinting the words in my brain. It was probably not appropriate to pull out my notebook right now to capture the new information. Jamie was Paula's son. Paula was Curtis's sister. Trying not to interrupt the exchange between Jamie and Curtis, I leaned slightly to Justin and out of the side of my mouth I muttered, "A new player. Remind me to add Jamie to my list."

Whipping his head my direction, Jamie glared at me, continuing his trek toward Curtis. Justin jumped up, holding up a halting hand. "Whoa."

Jamie clenched his fists and straightened his arms at his side, flexing his jaw muscles. He looked at Curtis and back at Justin. "Lucky for you," Jamie spat at Curtis, his nostrils flaring.

Justin, gently touching Jamie's arm, turned him away from the table. Allowing Justin to guide him, Jamie wobbled back to his seat a few tables away, chewing Justin's ear off the entire way. Good, hopefully more details for the story of what was happening to Paula. She appeared to be the center of attention for that family but was the one person not in attendance for the trip.

Curtis picked up his empty glass and held it to be served for the next round of tasting. "That little brat. He's just mad I didn't hire him as a driver," he said.

How some people had no qualms about airing dirty laundry was beyond me. It explained why many criminals got caught. Their arrogance, thinking they could get away with their crime, along with their stupidity for doing it in the first place, meant they would likely be nabbed by a good detective. I had learned from Barney, if you just leave a lot of silence, human nature is for people to fill it. And before you knew it, they slipped up with some juicy detail that did them in.

The final plates of food were served as the tasting was winding down, walnut- and blue cheese-stuffed mushrooms. The woman placing the food on the table must have gotten word about Curtis hogging everything and placed both trays as far from him as possible.

Huffing, Curtis hastily stood, his chair falling backward. He stomped around the table, clutching a handful of mushrooms for his plate. The smugness of that guy appeared to have no bounds.

Cathy averted her eyes from the spectacle of her husband, focusing on sipping her wine.

Justin returned to the table, his eyes wide. I hoped he had gleaned some new information from Jamie to help explain this mystery. We had a ways to go for this trip, and if we couldn't put the pieces together before it ended, someone might just be getting away with murder.

"I really like this one," Cathy said, scanning the group at the table. I nodded. "Curtis, I think we should order a case of this." Cathy smiled at her husband as she tried to lighten the tension.

"Sure, whatever you want," Curtis replied.

That guy had a split personality. Could his poor behavior be because he was under a tremendous amount of stress? We all acted differently in conflict, many times uncovering more of our true selves. Or was he always this boorish? I sincerely gave people the benefit of the doubt, knowing my own limitations and how pressure affected me.

Thankfully, we were nearing the end of this event. While I enjoyed the experience, I was dying to have time to compare notes with Justin and advance our theory of the mystery of Paula. The winery owner provided her closing remarks, thanking everyone for attending.

I grabbed my backpack from under my chair as we all rose from our table.

Cathy linked arms with Curtis as he stumbled toward the train. "Yeah, this was nice," he said.

Curtis's idea of nice was certainly warped. I couldn't imagine how the rest of this excursion would play out.

Justin navigated us toward Unkie and Linda, who looked like they were on top of the world. Linda's suggestion that Uncle Jack would enjoy this trip was quite insightful. The two of them appeared to be getting closer all the time, prompting me to conclude some type of union would be in their future.

CHAPTER SIX

The conductor guided the crowd onto the train for the next leg of our journey. A few days at our destination at the bed and breakfast should give us ample time to round up any clues, along with some rejuvenation. Our trip had a couple more hours remaining before the train deposited all of us for our overnight accommodations.

Glancing to my right, I saw Curtis and Cathy with linked arms boarding two cars ahead of us. Those two seemed to be the lynchpin for breaking this convoluted story wide open. I moved with the flow of the crowd to embark with my group. I hugged my backpack, ready to pull out my notebook and capture the events of the wine tasting. Jamie had entered the picture, certainly cementing the clues about Curtis not being a nice person. Jamie's accusation of him as the reason his mom had not come along on the trip with the rest of the family by itself didn't point to any wrongdoing, so I needed to peel the layers back and see what I could uncover.

I plopped into my seat next to Justin, anxious to get up again once the train was on its way.

Uncle Jack poked his head between the seats, his cheeks flushed. "I'm glad you two are here. This is such a wonderful trip," he said, extracting his head and gazing with a goofy teenage smile at Linda. My heart skipped a beat for him and Linda, feeling the love between them. "And we're just getting started," he said as he continued to beam.

Justin looked at me and snickered.

"I know," I said.

The train bumped along, gaining speed as it whisked us away from the winery. I wiggled in my seat, ready to explore. With Curtis and family a captive audience on the train, I figured we should get as much out of the situation while we could. Once everyone went their separate ways at the bed and breakfast, it might significantly harder to tail them. And time was ticking to find out what they were up to.

Scooting to the edge of my seat, I tapped Justin on his knee. Gesturing toward the aisle, I said, "Why don't we head to the dining car for dinner?"

He stood and held out his hand to hoist me from the seat. I didn't need the assist, but I accepted the thoughtful token. We waited for

Unkie and Linda to join us and filed ahead on our way to eat. Many of the passengers remained in their seats, apparently opting not to have dinner on the train. The bed and breakfast had offered a late meal due to our arrival time, but I couldn't wait that long. I certainly hadn't consumed as much wine as Curtis, but my stomach was rumbling for some nourishment that the hors d'oeuvres just couldn't satisfy.

Thankfully, there was a table for four open as we arrived. I slow-walked to my seat, glancing around to spot the subjects of inquiry. My shoulders slumped when I didn't see Curtis and Cathy. That's fine. We could enjoy a nice conversation with Unkie and Linda.

Justin held my chair for me as I sat. I snuck a peek at him, as he appeared to be smiling to himself. Until now, his and my relationship was as friends, companions on adventures, at least from my perspective. He was super easy on the eyes and quite the gentleman. Was he hoping for more? How in my dense skull had I not seen that before now? Probably because I couldn't let my heart strings out far enough to be tugged. My hurt from my ex was still relatively new. Was the romantic ambiance of the trip skewing reality? I did a double take of his expression. Nope, there was definitely something more there than just buddies. OK.

The waitress approached our table and brought water all around, and we all ordered coffee to begin. On the other side of the table I spotted Uncle Jack and Linda holding hands, Unkie leaning in to whisper in her ear.

"All right, you two. Seems like you've got a secret going on." I laughed.

Uncle Jack sat back. "Well, I guess we do. But for now, I'll just tell you we ordered a couple of cases of wine for a celebration when we get home," he said, cheeks flushed bright red.

I looked back and forth between them and then to Justin. "Do you know what they're talking about?" I asked him.

Shaking his head, he said, "I have an idea. But I'll wait 'til they're ready to share."

I playfully hit him on his shoulder. "Whose side are you on?"

The waitress interrupted our chat, brought our coffee, and took our order. I felt like I could eat a five-course meal. I had used all my energy in sleuthing Cathy and Curtis, though I was not sure I was any further along. Having Justin to bounce ideas off of and having another set of eyes would really help as we got to the bed and breakfast and everyone went their own way.

Just as the waitress left, Sandra arrived at our table and said, "Linda, I'm so glad we got a chance to meet at the winery." She stopped and looked at the rest of us, taking a step back. "I'm so sorry to interrupt. I'm just really excited with my idea."

"It's OK, Sandra. This is Justin, and Tilly is the owner of the bakery I was telling you about," Linda replied.

In my direction, Sandra said, "Nice to meet you." Returning her focus to Linda, she said, "I've been giving it a lot of thought. And I would like you to cater a celebration for Raymond when we get back home."

Linda looked at me and held out her free hand in my direction. "It's really up to Tilly. She's the boss."

Suddenly I was torn. My response was usually to say yes and ask questions later. That got me into trouble when I over committed, not considering the workload my current self was piling onto my future self. But in this case, if we needed to continue the sleuthing after our trip, the event would provide me the perfect opportunity to be up close and personal with this family.

Nodding, I said, "We'd love to."

Sandra placed her hand on her heart and tilted her head my direction. Her voice cracking, she said, "Thank you" so quietly I could only discern the words from lip reading. She wheeled around, almost toppling the plates being delivered by our server. She scooted to the side and returned to her corner table with Raymond, his back to us.

By all accounts, she seemed like a perfectly normal and nice person. How had she gotten hooked up with a family that had Curtis and

Cathy in it? Was there more to Sandra than met the eye? The age difference between her and Raymond was significant, but did that point to any evil intent on her part? If the business was truly doing well, and Raymond was willing it to his wife, had she married in expecting a windfall when he passed?

Pushing food around my plate, I realized my appetite had suddenly waned.

"She seems so nice," Uncle Jack said.

I looked at him to see if this was his usual snark or in fact if it was sincerity.

"It's a shame about Raymond. He seems pretty nice too," Unkie continued.

Glancing at Linda, I hoped an explanation for that comment was forthcoming. She must have seen the quizzical look on my face and said, leaning in and looking around, "Raymond has cancer. Only a couple months left."

Uncle Jack added, "Sandra is hoping for a family reunion of everyone before then. This trip was supposed to be it, but his daughter couldn't come."

Darn right she couldn't. And Curtis knew exactly why. If for no other reason, I now had to find out what happened to Paula for Raymond's sake.

CHAPTER SEVEN

Folding my napkin and placing it on the table, I turned toward Justin. "What do you say we head to the lounge car for the rest of the trip?" I looked at my watch, estimating about an hour remained before then. Sitting in the dining car wasn't getting us anywhere with this investigation.

"Don't make me have to wheel you off the train," Unkie chided.

"I'm just getting an iced coffee, you stinker," I said, needing my wits about me as we continued digging for dirt.

"That actually sounds really good," Justin said, standing and holding his hand for me again. Either he was really trying to get close to me or he thought my feeble body needed that much help.

I hesitated a split second, then grabbed his hand. From my peripheral vision I could see Unkie's eyes widen as he stared at us. I would not give him the satisfaction of acknowledging that response.

Letting go of Justin's hand as I left the table, I kept my eyes averted from Uncle Jack and followed Justin toward the lounge car. We traversed through several passenger cars until we reached the one near the end of the train. Bingo! Curtis and Cathy huddled in two overstuffed chairs in the corner. There were a smattering of others in the car, providing some coverage as we navigated to seats just close enough that we could hear their conversation--though Curtis bellowed loud enough we actually heard him before we even entered.

The table in front of Curtis and Cathy held two almost empty wine glasses, gently wobbling with the movement of the train. Being as large as he was gave Curtis an advantage in holding more liquor. But as much as he had at the winery, with so little food in his stomach, I was stunned he had continued to imbibe.

Justin and I took two chairs that left a small buffer between us and our targets. Curtis and Cathy didn't seem to notice our arrival, thankfully. The waitress took our order for the iced mochas, and I scooted my chair as close to Justin as possible. I was so glad there were two sets of eyes and ears to ensure we didn't miss any details of their conversation.

"Can you believe Jamie?" Cathy asked, her voice barking as if she were delivering a speech to a roomful of people. Justin and I could have probably sat in another car and still heard her.

Curtis bent over, retrieving his glass and emptying it. He grabbed the second one and did the same, holding it up to signal the waitress for refills. "Well, the apple doesn't fall far from the tree," he said.

I looked at Justin, who shrugged. Curtis was accusing Jamie of behaving the same way his mother had. From the confrontation at the winery, and knowing what little I did of Curtis, I was certain Jamie and his mom were standing in the way of something Curtis wanted. And he and Cathy appeared to do anything they could to get it. Was this still all about the business?

"He better be careful, or he'll meet the same fate," Cathy said, albeit a smidgen quieter. The waitress placed two full glasses on their table, removing the empties. She stopped at our table and delivered our drinks.

The arrogance of those two, hinting at something dangerous but not taking any care to keep it quiet. If I was planning or committing crimes I sure wouldn't broadcast it in public. But I expected that was part of the Achilles' heel of a criminal, thinking you're smarter than everyone else to the degree your ego blinds you to reality.

Cathy reached over and laced her fingers with Curtis's. "Everything is finally falling into place, baby. All that we've worked so hard for will soon be ours," she said.

Curtis tilted his head toward Cathy, smiling. "Just a couple more hurdles, but nothing I can't handle," he said.

If you walked in here right now and looked at the two of them, you would think they were a couple who just started their honeymoon. Gazing into each other's eyes, warm smiles, holding hands, all the indications of love. Sadly, I knew what was behind their facade of normalcy.

"That complication from Sandra was quite the blindside," Cathy said. She tucked her legs under her, leaning toward Curtis on the arm of the chair. Were we about to hear the backstory of Sandra and Raymond's marriage? Had Sandra known Raymond had cancer when she married him? Was her intent just as evil as Curtis and Cathy, only in competition with them for the business? Was that the meaning of Curtis's reference to hurdles?

"I blame Denise," Curtis responded. "If it wasn't for her and Paula's friendship, Sandra would never have met Dad."

I grabbed my drink and sucked in a long cooling swig. The proximity to those two couldn't have been more fortuitous to gain juicy details. Another player emerged onto the scene, apparently in the crosshairs of Curtis. He seemed to be lining people up that were between him and his goals and knocking them down like falling dominoes.

"I have faith in you, babe. Did you find out yet about his will? That's really the key to our dreams," Cathy said, ogling Curtis.

"Quit nagging me about that! Do you think I don't know? Seriously, I've got it handled. By the time we get back, Paula will be long gone without a trace. And my attorney will have all the paperwork we need," Curtis said. "Dear old Dad won't know what hit him."

Cathy squealed and clapped her hands, leaning in to give Curtis a kiss on the cheek. "And Maria goes. First thing," she said, wiping her hands like she was cleaning them. "Right?"

Curtis shrugged.

Cathy straightened her legs out from under her and stood in front of Curtis, hands on hips. "She goes, right?" Cathy said in a lower register, meaning business.

"Cath, she's a great office manager. She does a lot for this company, going above and beyond," Curtis said, his tone meeker than I had yet heard.

"That's the problem. Either she goes or I do. It's non-negotiable." Cathy dropped her arms to her side, clenching her fists. Were we about to see a scuffle right here on the train?

Curtis held out his arm. "All right. All right." He glanced our direction, acknowledging there were more people here than just the two of them.

Cathy flopped back into her chair, head down, pouting. "You know how much that bothers me," she whimpered.

Turning toward Justin, I asked, "Should we leave?" My concern increased that our presence near Curtis and Cathy would make it obvious we were tailing them. In public, at least, I hoped Curtis wouldn't do anything dangerous, but I didn't want to chance it.

"You're right," Curtis replied. "She's gone too."

Justin stood, and I scooted behind him, ready to distance myself from this conversation. The more I heard, the more confused and scared I got. Until now I wasn't afraid of harm, but if Curtis was willing to do whatever it took to get what he wanted, including getting rid of his sister, I didn't want to be standing in his way.

CHAPTER EIGHT

I practically speed-walked back to my seat, glancing over my shoulder to confirm Curtis wasn't tailing us. I shuddered and plopped down. Justin had a huge grin on his face, obviously enjoying the investigation.

"Justin, doesn't it bother you what they were talking about?" I asked.

Uncle Jack gave me a dirty look, peeking between the seats. I didn't blame him, hoping this mystery didn't break wide open and ruin his time with Linda.

"Tilly, what are they going to do in a crowd? It sounds like whatever happened was back at the wrecking yard," Justin replied. "Besides," he continued, patting my knee, "you've got me right by your side."

I pulled out my phone and tapped on the connection for the train Wi-Fi. Several seconds passed before I got a signal. I tapped on the internet search and elbowed Justin. "Do you know the name of the company?" I whispered, hoping not to alert Unkie to my snooping. I suspected he and Linda had their eyes closed, resting up before we arrived for the night at the bed and breakfast.

Justin shook his head. "Not sure if I heard it. Why don't you just put in tow company near Belle Harbor?" He pointed at my phone.

I typed in the search, and while it brought back results I grabbed my notebook and pen, handing them over to Justin. Dutifully he accepted them, ready to jot down any items of interest.

"That way, we can start with a small radius and expand as we need to." He tapped the pen to his temple.

Chuckling, I said, "Smart." So glad he and I were in this together. The search results finally displayed on my screen, with Harbor Towing and Wrecking right at the top of the list. There were others farther down that were outside of Belle Harbor. How would I find out which one was owned by that family?

Justin wrote the name of the business and said, "We could check out the state website for the business to find out the names of the owners."

"Before we do that, one more search," I said. Sure enough, looking for the largest tow company in the state brought up a similar list as the first search. Goosebumps popped up on my arms, and I quickly typed into the search to find the state's business website.

"Dang. With the internet, this is almost too easy," Justin said. "Maybe we could open our own detective agency," he suggested.

Not sure how it happened, but I did feel like I had a knack for this stuff. Somehow my brain seemed to have a need and an ability to connect dots in every situation. When something appeared to be a random event, my mind worked until it made sense to me. Plus, I was sure it wasn't as easy as going online to solve cases.

Inputting Harbor Towing and Wrecking into the state website provided all of the information registered for this business. Names of owners, locations, annual revenue, as well as claims against the company's bond. The business had been in operation for almost fifty years. And from the multiple pages of claims, quite a few customers were unhappy with the services provided. How could they ever stay in business with that many complaints? Several claims had been paid out, many over ten thousand dollars.

I showed the phone to Justin. He raised his eyebrows and started writing down the details. "Seems like they've got some shady business practices going too, for all of those claims," I suggested.

"Mm-hmm," he muttered. "I think we've heard quite a bit from Curtis and Cathy." Holding up the pen, he continued, "It would be interesting to talk with Jamie. Seems he's got quite a beef with them, and he's right in the middle of this mess."

"Ooooh, good one," I whispered. Uncle Jack stirred in his seat. I leaned closer to Justin. "And he didn't seem shy about expressing his feelings either."

"Yeah, under the right conditions, I think we could get him to crack this wide open." Justin sat back and closed his eyes too.

It had been a full day, no doubt. We needed to pace ourselves. We had quite a ways to go.

The sun appeared to be within an hour of setting into the ocean, the sky over the mountains to my left turning darker shades of blue, a few early stars twinkling. Away from the big city lights, the full night sky shone bright. The rhythm of the train lulled my body into relaxation, but my brain was still in overdrive. We weren't far from the bed and breakfast, where we would all go our own ways.

Curtis and Cathy had planned to attend the cider making, so we probably wanted to do the same. Jamie might be more inclined to do the stand-up paddle boarding, and I definitely wanted some quality time to snoop on him. Were Raymond and Sandra in on the scheme that Curtis and Cathy had going? Or did Sandra have her own shenanigans underway? And how was Denise tied into this twisted knot of drama?

The peace and beauty outside the window belied the angst inside the train. I reclined my seat back to gaze at the overhead sky through the windows on the roof of the train. The sound of the engine quieted as we neared the station at the bed and breakfast. Justin rolled his head toward me and smiled. I was glad he had agreed to come along on this trip, mostly so I wouldn't feel like a third wheel. Who knew I would need a partner for probing these odd circumstances we found ourselves in?

Before the train had come to a complete stop, the passengers popped up, ready to exit. The bed and breakfast had a very large house that over the years had been expanded to add rooms and a massive lodge to accommodate everyone staying for meals. Many of the guests would stay in rooms in the main building, but several would be in accompanying cabins on the property. I crossed my fingers that Curtis and family would be in close enough proximity so we could more easily keep tabs on them.

The crowd ambled toward our destination, lights blazing bright around the main house. The sun had just set, providing that transition between a light sky and the dark of night. Many more stars now flickered overhead.

I moved to the side of the crowd, signaling Justin to join me. I wanted to observe where Curtis and his family headed as we trailed the pack. I jerked my head in their direction. Justin gave me a thumbs-up.

As we neared the main building, several staff members mingled about with clipboards, simultaneously checking multiple people in at a time. I gladly waited at the end of the line to have the opportunity to get the lay of the land.

Curtis and Cathy had locked arms, more to prop each other up than any show of affection, I expected. I scanned the group to find the other family members, spotting Raymond and Sandra near the front. The staff member pointed them in the direction of the main building. Score. One more in the right direction. We quickly progressed to the front of the line, completing our check-in.

The entry of the bed and breakfast was the lodge where we would eat. From there, many hallways jutted on all sides to the rooms. The cathedral's open-beam ceiling was expansive.

From across the room, Unkie raised his arm to signal us to come over. "Hey, you two. We've got our rooms," he said, holding up card keys.

"Us too," I replied. "What do you say we meet down here at about seven for breakfast, then figure out what we want to do?" I suggested.

"I don't know how I'm going to choose. There's so many great things," Linda said.

"Maybe we'll just have to come back for another visit," Uncle Jack said, his eyes gleaming.

Those two had something up their sleeves and seemed to be enjoying their coy behavior. Another mystery on our hands that I was sure we would solve in time.

CHAPTER NINE

Despite the intense craziness of the day before, I was actually able to sleep like a log, hoping that would give me a leg up on the sleuthing for the day. The bed in my room was as soft as a marshmallow. I stepped over to the window and parted the curtains to welcome the morning. The sun was front and center, promising a warm day. I glanced down at my outfit, hoping my sleeveless pink shirt, plaid skort, and my charcoal Converse were appropriate attire for our day, whatever that turned out to be. The clock on the wall quietly ticked to 6:55 a.m. Time to head downstairs.

Many of the rooms in the bed and breakfast reminded me more of a college dorm room than a resort. I expected that had to do with trying to make space for as many people as efficiently as possible. Truthfully, it had all of the amenities that I needed. The shared bathrooms were large enough to accommodate several guests at once. Given my normal schedule of early rising, I had the place to myself. With extra time on my hands I had poked around online to see if I could flesh out the story of Curtis and family any further. I was able to confirm their business did financially very well, despite quite a few customer complaints and claims. I guess if you were in a desperate situation, needing your car towed, you'd take what you could get.

Opening the door, I headed toward the lodge for breakfast. The spread the owners put out from the looks of the brochure could feed an army. With so much to do, I guess they wanted you fueled up to enjoy the experience. As I neared the first floor, I heard quiet mumbles, the early crowd just waking up.

Uncle Jack and Linda stood at a buffet table along a wall, getting coffee. We made eye contact, and Unkie nodded.

Joining them, I said, "Good morning."

I would swear they were both glowing. Almost since the moment they'd met, they had become inseparable. I stepped around them and grabbed a cup, filling it from the giant coffee pot. We made our way to three seats at a very long table. The room could probably hold about thirty people at a time for a meal. Several small tables surrounded the centerpiece. The room was starting to fill, but I had yet to see Justin.

I sipped the hot liquid, feeling it awaken my body. "What's on the docket today?" I asked Unkie and Linda.

Uncle Jack deferred to Linda, who said, "I think we're starting off with the cider making."

"It would be fun to know how to do it, and maybe we could make some at home," Uncle Jack added.

Most everyone in the room began to take their seats, ready for the breakfast service. I swiveled my head, searching for Justin. Would I have to give him a wake-up call? While scanning the room, I also looked for any members of Curtis's family. Jamie was by himself at the coffee bar. Should I offer for him to join us? He was either a loner or ostracized by at least Curtis and Cathy. My heart went out to him with concern for his mother.

A woman about Cathy's age approached Jamie, engaging him in conversation, their voices quiet. Jamie peeked up from his coffee, gazing around the room. He turned his attention back to the woman, and they continued with their heads bowed toward each other.

Servers had begun to roam about, placing food along the center of the long table: bowls of fruit, containers of yogurt, plates of scrambled eggs, and bacon. But the dish that caught my eye was the coffee cake. Linda and I looked at each other at the same time, pointing to the platter with the pastry.

Laughing, I nodded. "Yes, I do think that would sell well at the bakery."

"I would love to try some samples to find the right one," she offered.

"You read my mind. Deal," I said.

I spotted Justin's golden locks as he emerged from the balcony and bounded down the stairs toward the coffee. He was such an outgoing guy and so easy to talk to. He joined Jamie and the woman, greeting them with a wide smile. Turning to browse the room, he acknowledged my presence and pointed our direction. Jamie and the woman headed our way, followed by Justin with his coffee.

"Sorry to be late," Justin said. "Those beds, though. Could have slept for several more hours."

Taking the seat next to me, he continued, "This is Tilly, Jack, and Linda."

We greeted them, and in return Jamie introduced himself and the woman as Denise, Sandra's daughter. Aha, the plot thickens with another member of the troubled family revealed.

Aha, an early start to digging our noses into their business. Unlike Curtis, Jamie seemed to be getting along with Denise. Perhaps we could get her to talk as well.

"This is quite some spread, huh?" Uncle Jack exclaimed.

We all nodded, dishing up our plates; my first choice was the coffee cake, front and center.

"May I have your attention, please?" A woman with a clipboard and nametag I couldn't read stood at the head of the table, glancing around the room. As we quieted down and focused on eating, she continued, "We have an extensive number of activities for you to join if you are so inclined. Or if you would just like to walk the grounds and enjoy the peace and beauty, we have several miles of trails."

She listed quite a few options, providing a variety of low-key to high-adrenaline choices. The guests continued eating as she described at least ten different things we could do. Two days here was definitely not enough time to enjoy everything.

I dished myself up a second piece of coffee cake, for research purposes, of course. The center was a creamy, buttery flavor with a cinnamon swirl. The top was loaded with a crunch topping almost as high as the cake was deep.

Unkie spied me from across the table and raised his eyebrows, his body bobbing up and down from his chuckles. The guests were finishing their breakfasts as the guide was directing them to their preference of activities.

My crew wrapped up, fueled for our morning of adventures.

"If you don't mind, I'd like to tag along with you," Denise said.

"Of course not. The more, the merrier," Unkie said. "Jamie?"

Falling in line behind us, Jamie said, "Nah, you go ahead." His head was down, his shoulders slumped. Why would you come to someplace like this and not participate? He seemed to have a lot on his mind about his mom.

"How about we catch up with you at the stand-up paddle boarding?" Justin offered. "Two o'clock?" He looked at his watch.

"I guess," Jamie said and ambled away toward the exit to the nature trails. Maybe a dose of peace and calm could snap him out of it. At least we might have a chance later with him by himself to delve more into his side of the story. Nobody in that family was shy about publicly declaring their position.

Glancing at Justin, then back at Jamie to see him disappear, I only hoped he showed up later.

CHAPTER TEN

The barn was a short walk from the main lodge. Ten of us had chosen the cider making as our first activity. We traversed the gravel path to the large open doors. As we rounded the corner to the opening, I spotted Curtis and Cathy in the far corner of the barn. Curtis's face was flushed as he quietly talked to Cathy. They both whipped their heads toward us as we arrived.

Coming in from behind us, the activity leader welcomed the group. In the middle of the space were several stations for each of us make our own batch. She directed us to select one and stand behind it. She moved to the center of the room and began describing the process we would use to make the cider.

Two down from me were Cathy and Curtis. I was close enough to hear them but not so close that they would get suspicious of my spying.

"At each of your stations, you have all of the supplies to make a batch of berry apple cider." The leader walked around the semi-circle, pointing to each item as she described its purpose.

With every new experience I had, I considered whether there was some way to incorporate it into my business. Homemade cider might sell very well. But creating it would be a time commitment, and I didn't have the time or the space for it. Perhaps another partnership in my future could offer cider that someone else made. Leaning over to Justin, I whispered, "Remind me to talk to Fiona about cider making."

"Got it," he replied.

My best friend's bar specialized in different types of tequila, offering a variety of signature cocktails that used the products from the local distillery. One of the things I loved about Belle Harbor was the homegrown feeling of the products-- that was another attraction for the tourists too.

Our instructor continued describing our process as we began to make our own jug of the juice. She brought around samples of different flavors for us to try as we continued the process. Just as with the wine tasting, Curtis glugged down the samples and asked for more.

That guy had a problem with alcohol. I scanned the room to see if anyone else observed the scene he was making.

"Figures," Denise muttered from my left.

Curtis whipped his head around, glaring at Denise. His look caused me to take a step back. I wanted nothing to do with this confrontation. Curtis made a noise that sounded like a growl. I looked at my watch. We had a few more steps to finish our batch, then I was ready to jet out of here. If I didn't see Curtis the rest of the trip, it would be too soon. "Why are you even here? You're not part of our family," Curtis said.

"You're not in charge of everything like you want to be," Denise replied.

Curtis slammed his jug onto the table. "Just you wait. You and your mom's scheme for her to marry my dad is going to backfire. The wheels are already in motion." Curtis tilted his head back with an evil laugh.

Denise sniffled, quietly saying, "Paula is my best friend. I just want her to be OK."

Justin and I simultaneously looked at each other. Had Denise confirmed that Curtis had done something to his sister? And what kind of scheme did Denise and Sandra have? Was there a plan to gain control of the business when Raymond passed away? With his death imminent, desperation appeared to be setting in. I just hoped I could piece together the mystery in time.

Nearing the end of our cider preparations, Justin and I wiped our hands on the towels and scooted toward the barn door. I thanked the leader, promising to come back to learn more for future reference.

When we were out of earshot of the others, I glanced over my shoulder and shuddered. "That guy is such a jerk!" I said.

Quickly moving down the path toward the water, Justin halted and grabbed my arm. "Got an idea. Why don't I sneak up to the rooms while you meet Jamie? I'll see if I can find out anything."

"Are you sure?" I asked. Secretly I wanted him to snoop. But what if he got caught? They might call the cops and haul him off to jail. Our whole purpose would backfire.

Justin bounced from foot to foot like a little boy excited for an adventure. I just hoped his exuberance wasn't clouding his judgment.

Glancing toward the water, I said, "OK. But hurry. I'll go get us a couple of boards and paddles for the lesson."

He turned on his heel and jogged toward the main building. My stomach churned with nerves. I followed the signs through the overgrown path to the lake. A few people were already kneeling on their boards, slowly guiding themselves around the water. I had seen this activity many times and had always wanted to try it.

I registered our names with the attendant, and he carried two boards with paddles to the water. "Wait here a few minutes until Rachel returns. Then she can get you guys going."

Nodding, I plopped down onto the nearby log. The time passing was probably close to ten minutes but felt like ten hours. I tapped my foot and focused on the people on the water, observing their paddling technique.

Oh, Justin. Why did I agree to that? Standing, I began to pace along the log. As I neared the end to turn, Justin burst through the opening from the trees, with Jamie in tow. How did that happen? I looked back and forth between them. "Hi Jamie. Glad you could join us."

"Me too," Jamie replied. His expression and his tone were more upbeat than earlier in the day. He headed toward the attendant to get his board and paddle.

I grabbed Justin's arm and pulled him close to me with a sweaty hand. "What happened?" I asked.

"It's fine. I happened to be in Curtis's room. I was coming out and Jamie was at the other end of the hall," Justin explained.

"Never again. That's too close," I said. Stepping close enough to Justin to feel the heat from his body I asked, "Well?"

Justin shook his head. "Not sure. I found a personal checkbook with a check to another wrecking yard for an exorbitant amount."

The attendant carried Jamie's board and paddle to join ours at the edge of the water. A younger, curly-haired woman fast-walked toward us. "You guys ready?"

Jamie stood near the water, waiting for us to join him. Would we be able to grill him at the same time we were paddling? Not knowing when we would have another opportunity, I had to take that chance.

We removed our socks and shoes and slowly placed our boards on the water, following instructions to kneel on them. Our guide explained how to balance ourselves to avoid going into the drink. Rachel navigated in between the three of us, showing us how to stand up if we wanted. For the time being, I was content on my knees. Justin and Jamie were bolder, both simultaneously standing and proceeding to topple into the lake. If nothing else, we were enjoying our time.

After climbing back onto their boards, they chose to kneel for a while longer to regain their composure. I anticipated this connection with Jamie could prove fruitful in our investigation in the mystery of the family. But we needed to move things along to strike while the iron was hot.

"Jamie, maybe someday we can meet your mom," I said.

His demeanor soured as he slapped the water with his paddle. No response.

I guided myself toward Justin, gesturing toward Jamie. Maybe he would have better luck. I probably went in too directly with my comment.

Justin sidled up to Jamie. "Thanks for joining us. Maybe we can hang out again before the trip is over."

Perfect. Lay the groundwork for future snooping. Both of them stood, attempting another shot at the actual stand up part of this activity. Rachel guided them each step of the way to a successful assent. I was content to stay kneeling as I paddled in bigger circles around the lake. Rachel followed me, encouraging me to attempt to stand. I was hesitant to create a spectacle and interrupt what I counted on was Justin's probing of Jamie for more clues. The two of them were getting the hang of this and were chatting up a storm. Go Justin!

CHAPTER ELEVEN

This morning, many of us were heading to visit the local Winchester Mystery House, a historic site with many curiosities. I would rather have chosen an outdoor activity, but Uncle Jack insisted this trip would be worth our while. Breakfast choices were largely the same as yesterday, with that homemade coffee cake as my go-to. I joined Unkie and Linda at the table as we nourished up for our trip.

"Where's Justin?" Uncle Jack looked around the room.

I stuffed my faced with the cinnamon delicacy and mumbled my answer. I could seriously eat an entire pan of this myself.

Thuds from the stairs prompted the entire room to turn their heads. Cathy had her rolling suitcase in tow. Was she leaving early? How would she get home since the train was to provide the return trip for everyone? If she was leaving, would Curtis join her? That would cut our investigation short and might mean we would never solve the mystery of Paula's disappearance.

"Why are you bringing that thing with you?" Curtis blustered. He stomped over to the side table with the coffee, Cathy trailing behind him. Did Cathy have something in there she didn't want anyone else to see? Was she somehow suspicious of Justin's poking around the day before? Had Jamie seen him and alerted Cathy? That last part seemed unlikely given the obvious strife between Jamie and those two.

Leaning in, Uncle Jack said, "I'm sure glad we don't have that family drama."

I nodded, launching into my second piece of coffee cake.

Justin appeared on the stairs, following Cathy and Curtis. Had he hung back to further snoop? We needed to debrief on his findings. Turned out he was a great partner, especially with his relaxed personality making people comfortable enough to spill their guts.

Our group leader arrived and beckoned us toward the bus, handing us each a sticker with a number on it. She explained it was an easy way to keep track of the group and ensure nobody got left behind. We all fell into line and headed outside.

"I told you, I didn't want to go. At least I'm bringing something to do that I enjoy," Cathy said as she juggled a coffee and her bag, Curtis not lifting a finger to help her.

What in the world did she have in that bag? We all filed onto the bus, Justin and I grabbing seats midway back, safely as close in proximity to Curtis and Cathy as possible. A row behind and on the other side of the aisle, Curtis and Cathy sat, her wheeling bag still in the aisle. The bus grumbled to a start and rolled on.

Our guide stood in the front and began describing the house to us over the loudspeaker as we rode for the short trip to our destination. The widow of the firearms magnate had purchased the eight-room farmhouse and began the most expansive, and in many cases, baffling architectural renovations until her death. The home boasted 160 rooms, two thousand doors, and all apparently without any plans whatsoever.

The bus stopped in the front circle driveway of the home to let us off. The enormous structure looked like a castle fit for a queen. I was unsure how we could tour the entire home in the limited time we would be here. We got off the bus and grouped together for our next set of directions. Our guide indicated we would split into smaller groups to more easily navigate through the house.

Glancing at Justin, I tipped my head in Denise's direction as the group splintered. He stepped toward Raymond and Sandra, leaving Curtis and Cathy on their own, her still lugging that bag with her.

Maybe one-on-one, Denise would open up a bit more. I eased up to her side and said, "Can you believe this place?"

Almost as if I startled her out of a trance, Denise jerked her head toward me, her eyes glazed. Where in the world was her mind? I slowly walked behind our group, urging her to join me. We turned left and entered through a grand doorway to begin the tour. No response from Denise. That's OK. We had time. We lagged at the rear of our group, listening to our guide and observing the oddities of the home.

Stopping at the staircase that went nowhere except up to a ceiling, I said, "I wonder why she did that."

"She was an odd duck," Denise replied.

Yes! A great start to getting her to open up. I needed to pace myself on the tour to attempt to get her to continue chatting before we were all done.

"Sad, she had no family when she moved out here from Connecticut and started this project," I said, steering the conversation.

The guide continued leading us through the many rooms of the house, pointing out the peculiarities along the way. Silence from Denise. Maybe buddying up to her was a bad idea. I was getting nowhere with any new information about the family.

"Yeah, sometimes I think about leaving everything behind and starting over," Denise said, running her hand along a banister.

Stepping close to her, I waited. Right on cue, she continued, "The drama of my family is relentless."

We ambled along at the tail of our group. No longer focused on the house, I was fully engaged with Denise. I needed to squeeze the most out of this time with her before the end of the tour.

"Seems like Curtis is an angry person. I'm sorry you have to deal with that," I said

Denise halted, her eyes bulging. "You have no idea the torment he brought on Paula." She shook her head, appearing in a daze. As our group navigated toward the exit, I held my arm that direction to prompt Denise to follow. "I'm actually glad Paula went on her own vacation. It's about time she stood up for herself."

The bright sun blinded us as we moved outdoors for the lunch on the lawn. Tables and chairs were set up along with cases of boxed lunches. If I could keep Denise talking during lunch, I might get even more dirt. I tried to guide her to a location far from the rest of her family.

On the far side of the lawn, Justin looked fully engaged with Raymond and Sandra. I tampered my excitement for the time being about hearing what he had learned. That guy could get anyone to talk about anything.

Denise plopped into one of the chairs at the end of a table. "Why don't I get us lunch and we can keep chatting?" I offered.

She shrugged. Was the well dry? I grabbed two bags and two bottles of water from the coolers and returned to my seat. Uncle Jack and Linda had buddied up at the other end of our table to another couple I hadn't seen before. Those two were having quite the adventure. Scanning the entire lawn, I searched for Curtis and Cathy--and the rolling suitcase. They were nowhere in sight as I stood and shaded my eyes, moving them methodically along the tables. That bag shouldn't be hard to spot, but for the life of me I couldn't find it. Curtis sat by himself mid-table on the other side of the lawn, the rest of the group giving him at least a couple of seats between him and anyone else. It wouldn't be a shocker if he had alienated everyone in his group during the tour. I swiveled my head. Where was Cathy?

CHAPTER TWELVE

While I had Denise by herself, and in somewhat of a talkative mood, I needed to wring out more details. "How do you know Paula?" I asked as I took a bite of my sandwich.

Denise pushed her food around on the table, lining up her sandwich, apple, and cookie. "We go way back," she uttered, continuing to arrange her food.

"Oh," I replied, tapping my foot. Time was ticking as she lumbered through answering my questions. I darted directly toward the target. "It sounds like she and Curtis didn't get along." Would my attempt be a home run or a strike out?

Denise whipped her head my direction. "That's a nice way to put it. Ever since Curtis was passed over for running the company, he's been sabotaging Paula to try and make her fail."

"That's sad. And with Raymond's illness, you would think the family would try to get along for his last days," I said. I gulped down some water to pause for her response.

"It's been the opposite. Fighting tooth and nail for the money. I don't really know what Raymond's will looks like, and I'm not sure anyone else does either." Denise bowed her head, nibbling a bite of her sandwich.

The tour leader stood and moved to the center of the group, informing us we had about ten minutes before we needed to board the shuttle for the return trip.

"I try to stay out of it as much as possible," Denise continued. "When I get back, I'm going to talk with Paula to see what can be done to secure her position in the company. I can't imagine it getting worse, but when Raymond passes, I think this lead-up to his death will look like kids play."

What lengths would people go to for greed and power, blindly forging ahead to remove anyone in their path?

Our guide gave the signal for us to head to the bus. Gazing around again and circling the group, I was certain Cathy was not here, and Curtis didn't have that rolling bag with him. I wondered about Curtis's motives. Was there something in the bag that they needed to dispose of? What would that be? It wasn't large or heavy enough to be a body. I gasped, and my hand flew to my mouth. I looked around, hoping I hadn't just concluded the actual results of the mystery of Paula. Were there body parts in there? Maybe Curtis and Cathy had several bags, and they planned to get rid of them along this trip?

I shivered. The evil that arose in some people was shocking.

Curtis strode past me with a confident swagger as he boarded the bus, sans Cathy. I followed as closely as possible, unsure what else I could discover at this late date on our return trip. Curtis returned to the same seat he and Cathy had on the ride over, his arm arrogantly stretched along the seat, preventing anyone from joining him.

Justin boarded the bus and joined me, grabbing my arm and leaning in. "Got some juicy stuff," he whispered.

Raising my eyebrows, I nodded. "Me too."

Running over the conversation with Denise in my mind, I repeated the key points so I would have them when Justin and I could swap notes. I was convinced Curtis was the mastermind behind this mystery, but we still needed the smoking gun. All of the innuendo, accusations, and motive didn't mean we had a clear-cut case. But was there enough for a police investigation? The story sounded like a plot from a movie of the week, but many times truth was stranger than fiction.

The bus pulled into the parking area and our guide explained the train would depart in thirty minutes for our return trip.

Justin and I sped toward the lodge. He turned and gestured for me to follow him into his room. "We don't have much time," he started. We quickly ascended the stairs and shut the door to his room. He paced, talking a mile a minute, quite out of the norm for that chill dude. His head was bowed as he focused on his story. "Raymond is planning to change his will, leaving Curtis out of it. Not only won't he ever be running the business, he's likely going to soon be out of it."

I gasped and stood, watching as Justin continued to pace. "Denise confirmed the conflict between Curtis and his sister. From her description, it sounded like Curtis was desperate and might do anything he could to get Paula out of the way."

Justin stopped, frowning, his eyes wide. "Tilly, I don't think we have much more time, only a few hours before the trip is over."

"Agreed." I ran for the door to gather my things. "I'll see you downstairs." Still not comprehending where Cathy had disappeared to, it occurred to me maybe she had opened her mouth one too many times for Curtis. Was there any way he had done something to her at the mystery house? Could he have done her in and stashed her in one of those truly odd locations in that twenty-thousand-square-foot mansion? It might take some time before anyone found her. I grabbed my stuff and raced downstairs.

The entire group was heading toward the train. I stood on my tiptoes looking for Cathy, not seeing her or Curtis. My heart lurched into my stomach. I felt the finality of this mystery slipping away.

Justin ran up behind me and we hurried toward the train. Without a word we hastily moved through several passenger cars until we arrived at the same one with Curtis. Breathing heavily, I collapsed into the seat, shoving my backpack under the chair in front of me. Justin heaved my bag up above to the luggage rack. We were one row back across the aisle from Curtis, the best vantage point we could have. He stood and opened the window next to his seat, rummaging in the suitcase on his seat. He lifted his eyes, looking around, and moved the suitcase next to the window. Was he about to chuck that out? What was in there that might incriminate him? If that bag went out when the train was at full speed along the cliffs, someone might never find it.

The train jolted forward, starting our return trip home. I elbowed Justin as I retrieved my notebook. We had a lot of ground to cover in a short period of time. Could we put the pieces together in a way that made sense? A lot of crazy, disparate facts and horrible family drama did not implicate someone in a crime. Turning to the page with my notes, I added Denise and Jamie and linked them into our diagram. Jamie was certainly disgruntled with Curtis, but did he have valid reasons to suspect something happened between his mom and Curtis? And Denise wasn't a neutral party with her mom married to Raymond. I shook my head to position my thoughts from emotional to a factual neutral position.

Taking Curtis's side for just a minute, I asked myself if he was just a giant bully; would that be enough to turn everyone against him, making it appear as if something nefarious had happened? Was he just an easy target to blame for the family issues? And what if he was right about motives of others trying to get him out of the business? I had to consider all angles to make sure he wasn't being railroaded.

CHAPTER THIRTEEN

My phone buzzed in my pocket. It was likely one of two people, either my bestie Fiona checking in or Barney with some news. Hesitantly I had called Barney about the cryptic story that was unfolding on our trip, my gut telling me it was more than just nutty family dynamics. Barney was very familiar with the Belle Harbor towing business, as they got a lot of calls from him for illegally parked town visitors. He didn't let on his feelings toward Curtis, but I inferred he just chalked up Curtis's demeanor to that of a crusty truck driver.

Barney's text said "You're on to something. Hang tight." I showed Justin the phone and he nodded. I typed back "We have a lot more to share when we return."

Glancing at our notes, I knew the picture was forming with Curtis at the center of the situation. I really hoped Barney was able to connect the dots that continued to evade me. I was certain if I had more time, I could uncover the final pieces.

Staggering from the front door of our car, Cathy appeared, face pale, bracing herself against a seat. She wobbled over and collapsed into the opening next to Curtis. "Never again," she said.

"I told you not to drink that second batch of cider," Curtis said. "The fermentation wasn't set and you have a weak stomach."

Cathy held up her hand. "You're right."

I looked at Justin. Shielding my mouth with my hand, I whispered, "Last time we saw her, she had that bag with her. I wonder what happened to it and what was in there."

Quickly I jotted down that note. The page with the diagram was cluttered with clues written in every open space. I turned the page and started a chronological list of what we had learned, when, and from whom.

"But it worked out. I didn't want to see that stupid mystery house anyway," Cathy continued.

"Whatever. I'm just glad this trip is about over." He clutched Cathy's hand. "We've got a new life ahead of us when we get back." Curtis's words dripped with sweetness, his demeanor completely changing before my eyes.

With only a few hours left before our arrival at Belle Harbor, Justin and I had to work fast to uncover anything else we could find. I pointed to our chart and Jamie's name. Justin nodded and stood. Hoping that bro connection could get Jamie to talk one last time, Justin headed off in search of any final clues.

I held my phone out again, pondering whether to text Barney anything more for now. It might take me quite some time to type everything out, and I didn't have any to waste. I tucked my phone in my backpack, moved it under the seat in front of me, and headed to the restroom.

Repeating the chronological events through my mind, I distractedly opened the restroom door to find the bag that Cathy had been wheeling around at the mystery house. Had she mistakenly left it there? Or was she trying to get rid of it? I reached to retrieve the bag and felt a shove from behind. I stumbled inside and fell to my knees, then pushed myself up, but another shove knocked me into the sink.

"You couldn't leave well enough alone, could you?" Cathy hissed. "We were home free with our plan until you and your boy toy came along." She had locked the door behind her. What was her game plan? To hold me hostage until we got back? That wouldn't keep me quiet, though. I gulped, quickly scanning her for an obvious weapon. Was this whole scheme Cathy's idea from the beginning? Did Curtis even know what she was up to?

"Help!" I yelled, trying to side-step Cathy toward the door.

She tipped her head back, cackling. "Nobody can hear you over the sound of the train." She had obviously thought this through.

I grabbed the bag from my side and thrust it at her, trying to get her off-balance. She caught it and pushed it right back at me, causing me to slip and fall into the corner.

"Help! Justin!" I screamed. I covered my head with my hands to ward off any weapon while I tried to devise an escape plan.

As Cathy stepped closer I grabbed her knees to take her to the ground. Only able to get one leg, I pulled and twisted with all my might, but I couldn't get past her to the door.

Taking a different tact, I said, "You'll never get away with it." I pulled the bag toward me and unzipped the main compartment.

Cathy grabbed my hand and pulled it away. Sticking my other hand inside, I really hoped I wasn't about to find something squishy and oozing. Instead, I retrieved a handful of papers.

"Get out of there," Cathy ordered, slapping my hand and returning the papers to the bag. "You don't know what you're talking about!" she screamed.

I only hoped at this point that someone else would need to use the restroom before our trip was over. If she had a weapon she intended to use to keep me quiet, it was hidden, giving me more time to escape.

"You were the one all along that plotted to get rid of Paula," I said. Maybe going right to the heart of the accusation would hit the target.

"Curtis was owed that company. He built it to where it is today, and that sick old man gave it to her instead," she said.

I made a quick move toward the door, hoping to reach the handle. If I could unlock it, maybe someone would inadvertently think it was unoccupied and enter. My hand braised the lock, just missing it.

"This is the end of the line for you," Cathy said, moving closer to me.

"Justin! Justin! Help! I'm in the bathroom!" I prayed he was back to our car by now and realized I was gone. Would he see my backpack still in our seat and conclude I was in the bathroom? Were his analytical skills good enough to notice both Cathy and I were missing?

Cathy booted me in the gut, causing me to lose my breath. This couldn't be the end of me. I had my new bakery and cafe to open. I had my new life in Belle Harbor to live. I had Unkie and Linda's wedding to plan, I hoped.

I bolted from the corner and tackled Cathy, banging up against the door. I scrambled to my knees as she pulled me from behind, my hand only inches from the door.

"Tilly?" I heard from outside. Justin's voice repeated, "Tilly? Are you in there?" He banged on the door.

"Justin, I'm here with Cathy!" I yelled.

"Unlock the door!" Justin yelled, banging furiously.

If only I could. Cathy had a death grip on me. I closed my eyes, reassured to have been discovered and willing Justin to break through and rescue me. Relief consumed me as it appeared Cathy had no weapon to disable me any further.

"I can't reach it!" I replied.

Relaxing against the strain of Cathy's grip, I knew it was just a matter of time before Justin would be coming through the door.

CHAPTER FOURTEEN

J ustin continued to pound on the door, ordering it to be opened immediately. After what seemed like an eternity, a foot permeated near the handle, splintering the wood. Jiggling the door and causing it to unlatch, Justin entered and Cathy released me and stood, wiping her hands on her skirt.

I bolted into his waiting embrace, burying my head on his shoulder. He held me out in front of him, looking into my eyes. "Tilly?" he inquired.

I shook my head. That ordeal had flustered me into silence. The pieces of the mystery were falling into place, but the trauma from being assaulted was just starting to take its toll. Justin wrapped me in his arms again.

Grabbing her bag and attempting to exit, Cathy said, "I don't know what happened. The door must have gotten stuck."

Justin let her by and whispered in my ear, "It's OK now. I'm here." We swayed slightly as Cathy squeezed by.

"But Justin," I started, swiveling my head toward Cathy, pointing her direction, all eyes on the spectacle.

His fingers interlaced mine as he led me back to our seats. Cathy had her bag in front of her, seated next to Curtis as the train slowed toward the station.

Justin gestured for me to sit, shaking his head so I knew not to make a scene. He was right. What good would it do to confront Cathy and Curtis on the train? Remembering my text to Barney, I grabbed my phone to see if there were any updates. Nada. Nearing the station, the train must have turned the Wi-Fi off. Did Barney send me a reply that I didn't get? What if Cathy and Curtis got away? Would they be able to escape arrest? They obviously had planned this out--did they have a liberation plan if things went south? Did they have money set aside and passports to leave the country?

Fidgeting in my seat, I drummed my fingers on my leg. The train slowly came to a halt. Justin and I stood as I tapped him on the shoulder, nudging him into the aisle right behind Cathy and Curtis. I whispered as quietly as I could. "Cathy said Paula's body is in a car in the wrecking yard, to be destroyed."

Justin reached back and squeezed my arm, nodding, as the crowd ambled toward the exit. Were we just going to let them walk away? After all this time I couldn't see that happening. "Justin," I pleaded.

Cathy turned her head ninety degrees, eyeballing us. They must have thought they were only steps to being home free. What could this nosy girl do to them? Not able to contain me in the restroom, I pondered if Cathy had other plans for me. What if she wasn't finished?

I ducked behind Justin for safety, hopeful for no other confrontations on the train. The group picked up a steady pace, leaving the train with the greeting of the conductor as we disembarked. I hopped down the last step and speed-walked with Justin as we followed Curtis and Cathy.

"Tilly," I heard Uncle Jack's voice from a distance.

I scanned the parking lot, looking for Barney or his deputy and their car. How could he not be here to greet the train? Did he not believe the story about Curtis and Cathy? I stopped. Was there a possibility I was wrong? And Curtis and Cathy were just mean people but did nothing else wrong? That couldn't be it. Cathy spoke of Paula's body. There were just too many unanswered questions.

Justin was now about twenty yards in front of me on the heels of Curtis and Cathy. My stomach fell. Cathy hadn't had a weapon, at least one that she displayed. But what about Curtis? If he did, Justin was walking right into the middle of it.

"Tilly." Uncle Jack continued to beckon me from a distance.

<u>All in good time, Unkie</u>. Thankfully, Justin and I hadn't burdened Uncle Jack and Linda with the details of our discoveries during the trip. I pondered whether to tell him about Cathy holding me hostage. That was probably better left unsaid.

Barney's police car barreled into the parking lot as his tires squealed. Curtis and Cathy glanced that direction and quickened their pace toward their car.

"Justin," I yelled and sped up.

He held up an arm and sprinted toward Curtis, knocking him into Cathy, the three of them tumbling like bowling pins. With Justin wrapping Curtis tight in his grip, Cathy stood, leaving her bag behind and running to her car.

I felt like I was watching an action-adventure movie at the last scene where the criminals were trying to get away from the cops. Barney's deputy raced from their car, grabbing Cathy's hand as she was inserting the key into the lock. He pulled her arm behind her and secured her wrist in handcuffs as she bent over the car weeping.

Behind them, Justin and Curtis wrestled as Barney approached. Pulling Curtis up by his elbow, Barney said, "I'll take it from here." He began reading Curtis his rights, arresting him for the murder of Paula.

Uncle Jack arrived at my side, out of breath. "Um, Tilly. Is there something you want to tell me?" The entire crowd from the train had joined the spectacle in a half-circle.

Justin rose to his feet and joined me, rubbing his elbow that had slammed into ground with the tackle. "It was mostly me, Jack," he said.

"I really doubt that," Uncle Jack replied, chuckling. "This one"--Unkie gestured toward me with his thumb--"can't resist solving a good mystery."

I wrapped my arm around Justin. "I'm just glad that you were there, or else..." I said, peeking at Unkie.

"Well, maybe I don't want to know," Uncle Jack said, chuckling. He reached for Linda's hand and brought it up for a gentle kiss, looking lovingly into her eyes. "We were too busy enjoying ourselves."

Barney and his deputy had placed Curtis and Cathy in the back of the police car and their bag into the trunk. "Justin, you OK? I can have medical come take a look at you," Barney said.

Rubbing his elbow, Justin said, "Nah, just a scrape. It'll be fine."

And possibly leave a scar bearing the memory of the takedown of a murderer. I shivered, thinking of all the different ways that could have gone. But all I needed were the people in front of me. One of these days I would have to take a truly relaxing trip. For now, I had a new bakery and cafe to open. Luna's was set to welcome the residents and guests of Belle Harbor in just a few days. My dream of opening my very own bakery like my grandma Luna was now a reality.

CHAPTER FIFTEEN

"Tilly, where do you want these?" Uncle Jack asked, holding out a stack of muffin pans.

Snickering, I said, "In the cabinet labeled muffin pans," and pointed toward the corner of the kitchen. Linda had suggested we label our drawers and doors to keep things organized. I don't know how I found such an organizational kindred spirit to be my assistant. Along with those skills, she was creative in the kitchen and had already brought along a few new recipes to add to the rotation of the bakery. She was kind, funny, and to boot, her and Unkie had totally hit it off.

After our train excursion, I was waiting for the other shoe to drop. They had hinted at an announcement, and I had to regularly bite my tongue not to pry, which totally went against my natural curiosity.

I stood back and wiped the moisture from my forehead. The help from Unkie, Justin, and Fiona to prepare for the bakery's opening looked like little elves getting ready in the workshop the night before Christmas. This endeavor was totally a team effort. Before my parents returned to Boston from their trip, they had guided the progress of the bakery to the point where we now only needed to fill the insides with supplies and food.

Linda and I chose only a few bakery items for the opening so that we could be sure we could keep up with demand. The cafe choices consisted of a salad and a wrap. Feeling pressure in my chest, I slid to the floor. Would we be able to pull this off after all? A tiny kitchen in Unkie's antique shop was manageable with the two of us. This new spot felt like orders of magnitude more. The overwhelm of the additional responsibility felt like a thousand-pound weight on my shoulders. If this didn't go well, it would be a spectacular failure. Pots and pans clanged as the crew continued to unpack our supplies. The kitchen gleamed with new equipment and a setup that would support an extensive production line, thanks to my dad.

Mom's design touches for the cafe portion made it look like old-world charm met chic but relaxed beach decor. With my hand on my heart, my pulse quieted. I really wanted my parents here to share in the accomplishment they helped to make happen. I would send them the newspaper article that the Belle Harbor Gazette promised they would do for the grand opening.

Justin approached and reached out his hand. I accepted and hoisted myself up, putting my arm around him for a brief hug. The din quieted and I stepped to the center of the kitchen. I inhaled deeply to avoid bursting into tears, my emotions right at the surface. "I can't thank you all enough for being part of making my dream come true."

Linda looked around and said, "We've made great progress. I think we've earned a break." She led us into the cafe toward a table.

Unkie, Justin, and I sat as Justin grabbed my hand under the table. Linda and Fiona stepped behind the counter.

"We didn't think it would be a celebration without a few treats," Linda said. She carried a tray of her signature millionaire salted caramel shortbread. And Fiona had a pitcher with glasses. "And I experimented and made a batch of that cider. I think I found a combo that works, and it turned out great!" They set the goodies on the table and joined us, serving everyone a round.

"I'm just glad we all made it back here alive," Unkie said, peering at me over the top of his cider glass.

"Don't be so dramatic. What could they have done with all of those people around? And Justin?" I said, squeezing the hand he continued to hold. I was keeping that scuffle with Cathy in the bathroom on a need-to-know basis with Unkie. Frankly, I wasn't sure if he would let me go from the antique shop if he knew how bold I had been in pursuing the truth. My only hope was that Barney wouldn't spill the beans. He brought both Justin and me into the office to get our testimony of events.

While Barney couldn't officially share details of an ongoing investigation, he graciously confirmed to us that sadly Paula's body had been found exactly where we thought. Curtis had scheduled for the destruction of the car where he had stashed her, the wrecking yard completely unaware of their part in almost destroying evidence. Cathy, as his accomplice, would no doubt spend an extensive amount of time behind bars. With both of them out of the picture, Jamie and Denise stood in line to take over the business. Through this tragedy, I only hoped the remaining family members could come together for healing. Perhaps their joint venture in the business could give them purpose to carry on after Raymond's death.

"Well, I expect this place will keep you busy enough for a while to keep you out of trouble," Uncle Jack said. "And," he started, and looked at Linda, "we have a little celebration of our own to share." He reached across the table and took her hand, smiling and gazing lovingly into her eyes. She nodded. Unkie slowly looked around the table at each of us.

"You're getting married!" I blurted. What else could it be? I really hoped I hadn't stepped in it right in front of everyone.

Uncle Jack nodded. "We wanted to wait until the time was right to tell you. I proposed to Linda on our trip."

How could I not have seen the ring on her finger before now? It was a rock and deservedly so. I moved to the other side of the table between Unkie and Linda with an arm around each and squeezed. The family was growing.

"And of course, I want to help plan the wedding." I smooched Uncle Jack's cheek, wiping my tears as I returned to my seat. The emotions of the recent events bubbled over.

"I hope those are happy tears," Unkie said.

I lifted my cider glass. "To Uncle Jack and Linda. May you have many happy years together." We all raised our glasses and saluted the couple.

A knock at the door startled me. We clearly weren't open yet, even though our sign was out. The door was closed and the outside lights were off. I approached and saw the reporter from the Gazette outside. Maybe I miscommunicated the opening schedule.

"Hi Robin," I said, opening the door. "We're not open yet."

"I'm sorry." She looked at her watch. "I must have misunderstood. I can come back tomorrow." She turned to leave.

"Wait." I looked back at Unkie and Linda. "While you're here, you could get an exclusive about Uncle Jack and Linda's engagement for the announcement section of the paper."

"Really? I never thought the day would come," she said, entering.

"You and me both, Robin. But when the right person comes along, it's out of your hands," Uncle Jack said, rising and giving Linda a hug.

From the corner of my eye I saw Justin's face expand into the biggest grin. My pulse quickened again. That curly-haired guy had captured my heart. I couldn't wait to see where this next adventure would take me.

WHAT'S NEXT? BONBONS AND BODIES

*G*ummed up game time, hat tricks, and grounds for murder...

Eighth in the Belle Harbor Cozy Mystery series!

Tilly and her assistant are in high gear with the grand opening of the new cafe and bakery. Add a new love interest into the mix and she feels like she is now unstoppable on the road to her dreams.

With her pro baseball brother's team in town, Tilly escapes for a few hours with her new boyfriend to cheer him on. Just as they settle into their seats, the team goes down by six runs. The coach trots out to the pitcher's mound to make a change and keels over dead.

Tilly's brother finds himself in the middle of professional sports jealousy, back-stabbing teammates, and twists and turns reminiscent of the best pulled salt water taffy. Can she solve the mysterious death of the baseball coach or will her brother be forced to hang up his glove for good?

Get Bonbons and Bodies from Amazon and start reading right away!

Sneak Peek of Bonbons and Bodies

"You know, I think turnabout is fair play," David said as we continued our leisurely stroll.

I knew darn well where he was going with this, the little stinker, but I wouldn't bite. "We need to stop by Unkie's sometime soon too," I suggested, planning to invite Uncle Jack and Linda to David's game before the team left town.

"Nice try. So Justin," he said.

We stopped just inside the front of the hat store, several silly, whimsical choices in the display window beckoning us to try them on.

Ignoring David's prompt, I grabbed a floppy, teal-colored hat with fuchsia feathers standing up and placed it on my head. "Am I ready for the Kentucky Derby?" I asked, glancing in the mirror.

David reached for a black pirate hat with a white skull and cross-bones on the front and black braids draped down the sides. "Argh, matey," he growled in his best pirate voice. This adventure was most definitely easing the tension for him. Mission accomplished. He returned the hat to the display. "Still waiting for your answer," he prompted. Grabbing a tall, red- and white-striped Dr. Seuss Cat in The Hat, he pulled it down around his ears and shook his head for the hat to jiggle.

Winding our way further into the store, I grabbed a 1920s hat, described as a flapper cloche. The knit crotched cream-colored hat held a large flower on the side with a shining pearl accent. Not something you would likely need in Belle Harbor. Placing it on my head, I glanced in the mirror as it covered most of my short hair.

"All right. Yes, we're something. But I'm not exactly sure what yet. Are you happy?" I softly punched him in the arm.

"Are you happy?" he asked with all seriousness. "That's all I want to know."

David grabbed a fedora companion to my flapper hat and pulled out his phone for a selfie with me.

"Yes. And send me that pic please."

We returned our hats and quietly worked our way to the exit, trying on several more styles. If I stopped for a bit to think, I realized I was very happy. My new life in Belle Harbor had everything I had ever wanted. The cafe was booming. Uncle Jack and Linda were engaged and my closest family. My bestie Fiona was a riot and partner in sleuthing. And Justin. For now, I kept my expectations low. I didn't want to be disappointed, but I was hopeful for the possibilities. We were friends before we started getting more serious, so I knew I really liked him. He was kind, a hard worker, and if I allowed my mind to wander, I honestly could see myself with him for the rest of my life.

My heart fluttered at my thoughts as I realized David was nowhere near me on the outside of the store. Deep in my thoughts, I had wandered away from him. I glanced throughout the mall to find where he had gone. He must still be in the hat store. Maybe he couldn't resist that pirate hat. The guys would get a big kick out of that.

I reentered to find him staring at one of his team's baseball caps in his hands. "David?" I asked. I hoped our adventure wasn't about to abruptly be cut short with a return to the ominous subject of Ernie's murder.

"What?" he asked, snapping out of his trance. "Oh, Tilly. What did you say?" He slowly placed the cap on the display mannequin.

"Let's head out and eat our lunch," I suggested.

He didn't move, shaking his head, clenching his fists. I so wished I could take his pain away. "There's just something not right," he mumbled, continuing to stare at the hat. "I didn't realize it until now." He slowly turned his head toward me, intently staring like he was trying to impart his thoughts.

"What are you talking about?" If he was open to discussing the subject, I was all in for him. Until this was solved it didn't seem like he would have much peace.

He grabbed the hat again and held it out to me, pointing at the bill. "Do you see this emblem where it shows it's official team gear?"

I nodded, no clue where he was going with this.

"Randy's hat at the game the other night didn't have that," he blurted, shaking the hat at me.

Still not following, I replied, "So?"

"So," he said. "Why would he be wearing a non-sanctioned hat?" He shook his head, replacing the hat and heading for the exit. Just outside the door, he turned and said, "Tilly, I really don't want to think Randy had anything to do with Ernie's death." He turned to see who was nearby and stepped closer to me, lowering his voice. "But nobody knew better than I did how much he hated that guy."

Get Bonbons and Bodies from Amazon and start reading right away!

Sue Hollowell is a wife and empty nester with a lot of mom left over. Finding a lot of time on her hands, and as a lover of mystery novels, she began telling the story of a character who appeared in her head.

The Chemical Bond is a book about Meredith Markette, a young woman who reluctantly enters into the field of law enforcement when her police officer father is killed in the line of duty. Her quest is to discover his murderer and in the meantime come to terms with a tragedy of her youth.

Will this book ever see the light of day? Maybe. Sue really likes the story and character. And writing that book taught her a ton about the publishing industry. Through this experience she has discovered a love of writing stories, and especially mysteries. She hopes you enjoy her books as much as she enjoys writing them.

Connect with Sue on Facebook at www.facebook.com/sueh ollowellauthor and sign up for her newsletter to stay in touch with all things cozy!